# Fishy Friend

Written by Kipp Whysall
Illustrated by Anni Axworthy

## Collins

Sam and his family went to the beach with a net, a spade, and a bucket each.

Mum built a sandcastle,
Dad dug a moat,
Sam fetched the water
and Tom sailed his boat.

They needed one more bucket
to fill it to the top,

But then something pinched Sam,
and that made him stop.

A cheeky crab had crawled along
and nipped him on his toe.

Sam bent down and picked it up,
smiled and said "Hello!"

Sam and the crab played in the sea,
they laughed and splashed together.

But then the tide came in and washed the crab away forever.

Sam searched and searched among the waves but couldn't find his mate.

"Time to go now," said Mum,
"It's cold and getting late."

At home Sam emptied his bag ...
And, clinging to his jeans,

He found his friend the cheeky crab,
Who joined him for baked beans.

# Sam and the crab

# 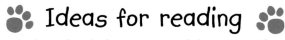 Ideas for reading

Written by Linda Pagett B.Ed (hons), M.Ed
*Lecturer and Educational Consultant*

**Learning objectives:** recognise automatically an increasing number of familiar high frequency words; visualise and comment on events, characters and ideas, making imaginative links to their own experiences; make predictions showing an understanding of ideas, events and characters; tell stories and describe incidents from their own experience in an audible voice; create short simple texts that combine words with images

**Curriculum links:** Geography; Citizenship

**High frequency words:** his, one, then, that, made, him, had, but, could, not, home, who

**Interest words:** moat, crab, nipped, forever, baked beans

**Resources:** whiteboard

**Word count:** 155

## Getting started

- Demonstrate telling a story from your own life experience which involves holidaying on the beach and then encourage children to swap theirs. Discuss activities that take place there, e.g. swimming and building sand castles.

- Using the whiteboard, draw a picture of a bucket and, as a group, fill it with words from the seaside, such as seaweed, bucket, spade, castles.

- Introduce the story by reading the front and back cover with the children, then ask them to predict who Sam's new friend might be.

## Reading and responding

- Encourage children to read pp2–3 together and identify the rhyming words.

- Direct children to read independently to p5 and then ask them to predict who they think had pinched Sam.

- Encourage children to read to the end of the poem prompting and praising for decoding tricky words.

## Returning to the book

- Using pp14–15, encourage children to retell the story as either Sam or the crab, using expression.

- Return to children's predictions. Was anyone correct? Discuss children's reaction to finding out that it was a crab that had pinched Sam, and whether they were surprised.